P9-CQX-043

TITCH

by PAT HUTCHINS

Aladdin Paperbacks

Aladdin Paperbacks
An imprint of Simon & Schuster
Children's Publishing Division
1230 Avenue of the Americas
New York, NY 10020
Copyright © 1971 by Pat Hutchins
First Aladdin Paperbacks edition, 1993
Printed in the United States of America
30 29 28 27 26 25 24 23 22 21

Library of Congress Cataloging-in-Publication Data
Hutchins Pat. 1942-
 Titch / by Pat Hutchins
   p.   cm.
 Summary: Titch feels left out because he is so much smaller than his
brother and sister until he gets a little seed that grows bigger than anything
they have.
 ISBN 0-689-71688-5
 [1. Size—Fiction.   2. Brothers and sisters—Fiction.]   I. Title.
PZ7H96165Ti   1993
[E]—dc20   92-1642

For Darren

Titch was little.

His sister Mary
was a bit bigger.

And his brother Pete
was a lot bigger.

Pete had a great big bike.

Mary had a big bike.

And Titch had a little tricycle.

Pete had a kite
that flew high
above the trees.

Mary had a kite
that flew high
above the houses.

And Titch had a pinwheel
that he held in his hand.

Pete had a big drum.

Mary had a trumpet.

And Titch had
a little wooden whistle.

Pete had a big saw.

Mary had a big hammer.

And Titch held the nails.

Pete had a big spade.

Mary had a fat flowerpot.

But Titch had the tiny seed.

And Titch's seed grew

and grew

and grew.